Dan Taps

Written by Tina Pietron

Illustrated by David Hurtado

Collins

Tap it.

Dad naps.

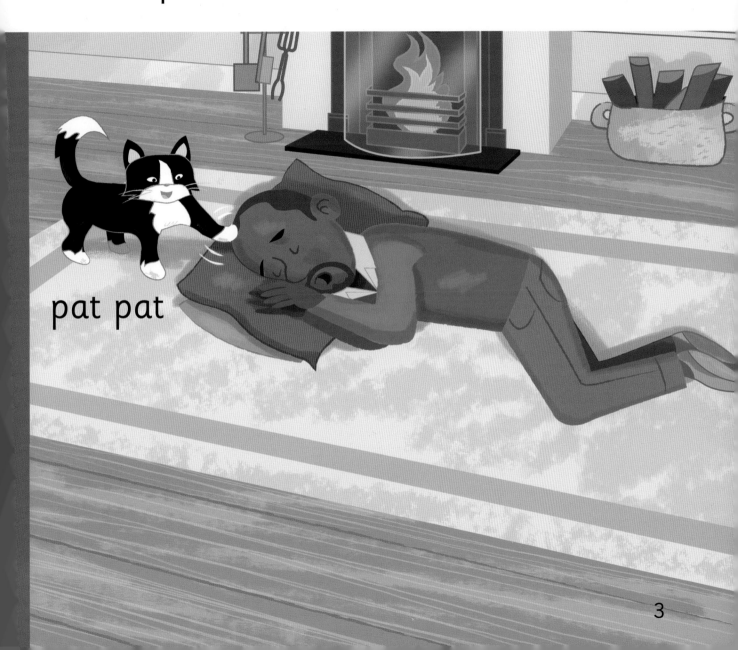

pat pat

Tap it.

tap
tap

Dad naps.

nap nap

Tap it.

tap
tap

Nan taps.

tap tap

Tap it.

tap
tap

Nan taps.

tap tap

Dan sits.

Dan pats.

pat pat

Nip in.

sit sit

13

14

🐾 After reading 🐾

Letters and Sounds: Phase 2

Word count: 48

Focus phonemes: /s/ /a/ /t/ /p/ /i/ /n/ /d/

Curriculum links: Personal, social and emotional development

Early learning goals: Reading: use phonic knowledge to decode regular words and read them aloud accurately

Developing fluency

- Your child may enjoy hearing you read the book.
- Take turns to read either the main text or the text in the pictures.

Phonic practice

- Turn to page 7 and point to the word **Nan**. Ask your child to sound out and blend the letters in the word. (N/a/n – **Nan**) Turn to page 10 and repeat for **Dan**. (D/a/n – **Dan**)
- On pages 4 and 5, focus on the words **tap** and **nap** in the picture. Ask your child to sound out and blend each. Ask: Which two letter sounds are the same in each word? (/a/ and /p/)
- Look at the "I spy sounds" pages (14–15). Point to and sound out the /d/ at the top of page 14, then point to the dog and say "dog", emphasising the /d/ sound. Ask your child to find other things that start with the /d/ sound. (*dinosaur, Dan, donkey, Dad, dining room, dress, dots (on Grandad's jumper)*) Next point to the pudding and say "pudding".
  Can your child hear the /d/ sound in this word? Repeat for "Grandad".

Extending vocabulary

- Turn to pages 6–7 and read the sounds that Dan and Nan are making. Ask your child: What other words could you use to describe the sounds? (e.g. *bang bang, knock knock; clack clack, clop clop*)